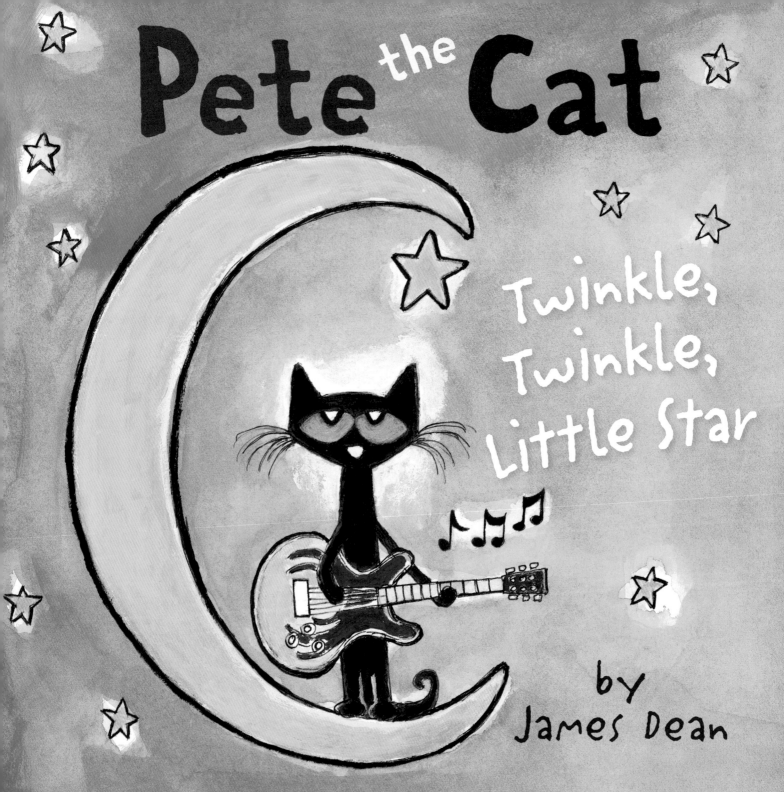

Pete the Cat

Twinkle, Twinkle, Little Star

by
James Dean

HARPER

An Imprint of HarperCollinsPublishers

ISBN 978-0-06-230416-2

The artist used pen and ink, with watercolor and acrylic paint, on
300lb hot press paper to create the illustrations for this book.
Typography by Jeanne L. Hogle
14 15 16 17 18   LP   10 9 8 7 6 5 4 3 2

First Edition

Twinkle,
twinkle,
little star,

How I wonder what you are!

Up above the world so high,

Like a diamond in the sky.

When the blazing sun is gone,

When he nothing shines upon,

Then you show your little light,

Twinkle,
twinkle, all the night.

Then the traveler in the dark,
Thanks you for your tiny spark.

He could not see which way to go,
If you did not twinkle so.

In the dark blue sky you keep,
And often through my curtains peep,

For you never shut your eye,
Till the sun is in the sky.

As your bright and tiny spark,
Lights the traveler in the dark.

Though I know not what you are,

Twinkle,
twinkle,
little star.

Twinkle, twinkle, little star,

How I wonder what you are!

Up above the world so high,
Like a diamond in the sky.

Twinkle,
twinkle,
little star,

How I wonder what you are!

How I wonder what you are!